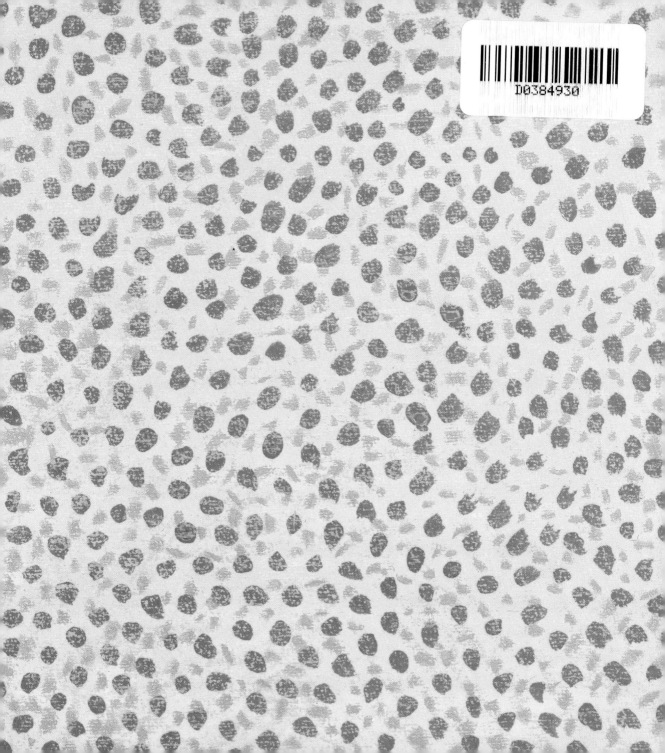

D.W., Go to Your Room

Marc Brown

#39778789

Little, Brown and Company
Boston   New York   London

For my little sister, Kim

First Edition

Based on a teleplay by Kathy Waugh

Library of Congress Cataloging-in-Publication Data

Brown, Marc Tolon.
    D.W., go to your room! / Marc Brown. — 1st ed.
        p.   cm.
    Summary: When D.W. is sent to her room as punishment for
  making baby Kate cry, it is Kate who finally makes her feel better.
    ISBN 0-316-10905-3
    [1. Sisters — Fiction. Family life — Fiction. 3. Aardvarks —
Fiction.] I. Title.
PZ7.B81618Dwp 1999
[E] — dc21   98-42841

10 9 8 7 6 5 4 3 2 1

WOR

Printed in the United States of America

It was cold and rainy outside. Inside, D.W. was playing with her blocks.
"This is *my* castle," she said.
"Glooba," said baby Kate.
"Don't touch!" shouted D.W. "This is *mine*."

Baby Kate took a block and laughed.
"Now look what you did!" yelled D.W.
"D.W.," warned Mother.
"She took my block," said D.W.

"Kate is a baby," said Mother, "and you're a big girl."
"I'm not a big girl," said D.W. "I'm a little girl."

Baby Kate took another block and giggled.
"That's it," said D.W., trying to whisper. "Give it back,
or I'll pinch you!"
When D.W. grabbed the block, baby Kate began to cry.

"Dora Winifred Read! Go to your room!"
ordered Mother.
"What did I do?" asked D.W.

In her room, D.W. stomped around. This is so unfair, she thought. I'm a prisoner in my own room!

"How will I survive?" she called downstairs. "I could starve."

"Dinner's in ten minutes," said Mother. "You can come out then."

D.W. looked at her clock.
It's not moving, she thought. It must be broken!

But when she went downstairs, Father wouldn't listen.
"D.W., go to your room," he said.
"Okay, okay," said D.W. "You don't have to treat me like
a criminal."

Back in her room, D.W. felt sorry for herself.
I'm just a little servant girl for Mom, Dad, and Arthur,
she thought. All I do is work, work, work.

Nobody loves me, thought D.W. And it's all Kate's fault!
Maybe we could sell Kate at the next yard sale.

Nobody loves me, thought D.W. And it's all Kate's fault!
Maybe we could sell Kate at the next yard sale.

Suddenly D.W. remembered that her new bike was out in the rain.

She ran downstairs and into the kitchen.
"The only bike I have in the whole world is outside in the rain!" she cried. "It's getting rusty!"

"I'll put it away," offered Arthur.
"Okay," said Mother. "D.W., go to your room."
"Will the punishment never end?" moaned D.W.

Grandma Thora is the only one who really loves me,
thought D.W. Wait until I tell her what they did to me.
She'll fix them.

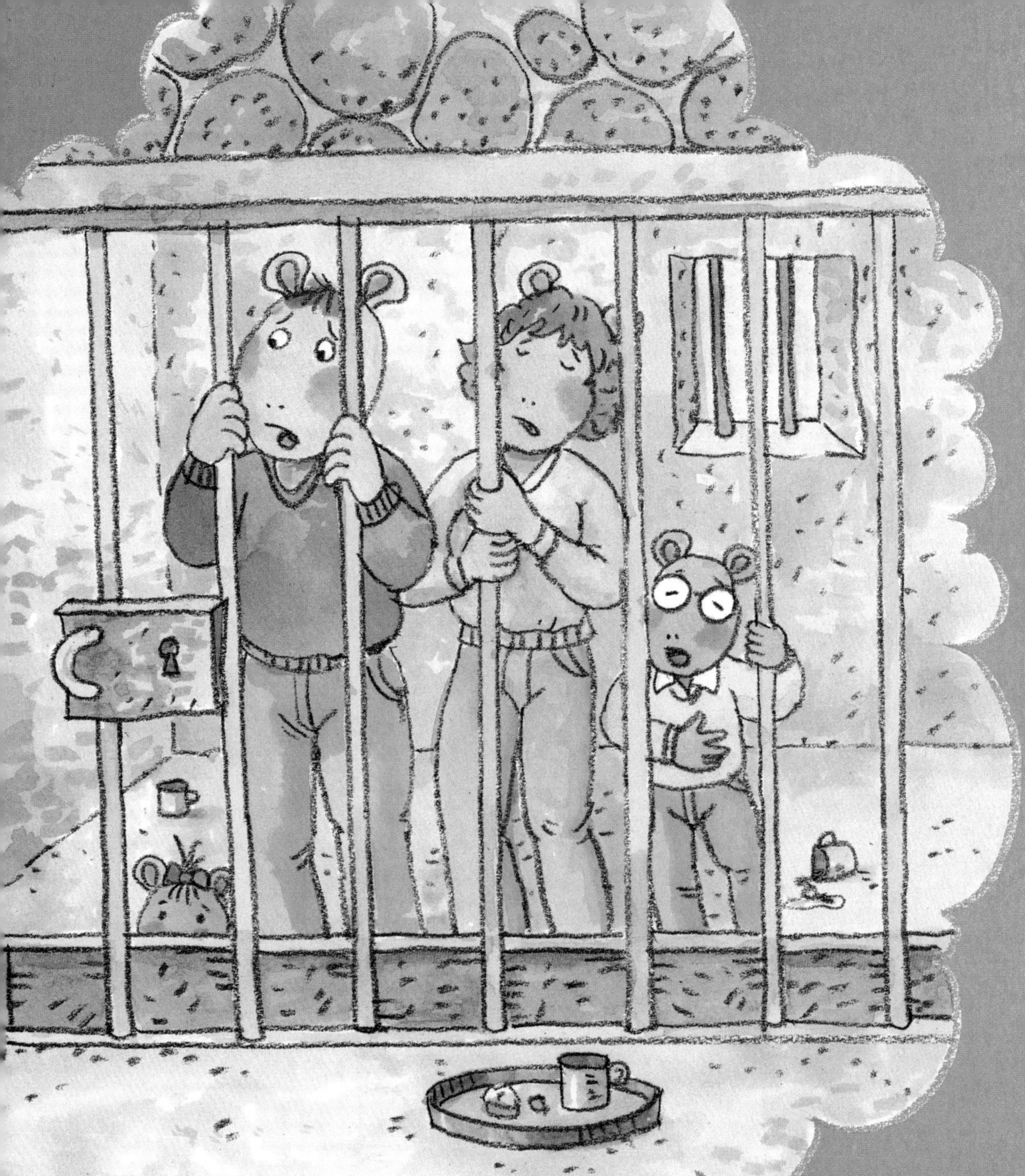

Then D.W. got an idea.

I'll run away and go live on Button Island all by myself,
she thought. Then they'll be sorry.

D.W. was packing when Mother came in with baby Kate.
"Hi, sweetie," said Mother. "Would you watch Kate for a
minute?"

"First I'm punished," said D.W.
"Now I have to baby-sit the enemy!"
Kate giggled.

"Don't smile at me," said D.W. "This is all your fault."
Kate laughed and offered her pacifier to D.W.
D.W. looked at Kate.
I must be the meanest sister in the whole world, thought
D.W.

She gave Kate a hug.
Just then, Mother came in.
"Now, that's the D.W. I like to see," she said. "By
the way, your time-out is over. Dinner's ready."
"Dinner?" said D.W. "But we want to play awhile."

"Dinner's getting cold!" called Mother.
"We're playing dolls," called D.W. "Just five more minutes? Pleeeeeeease?"

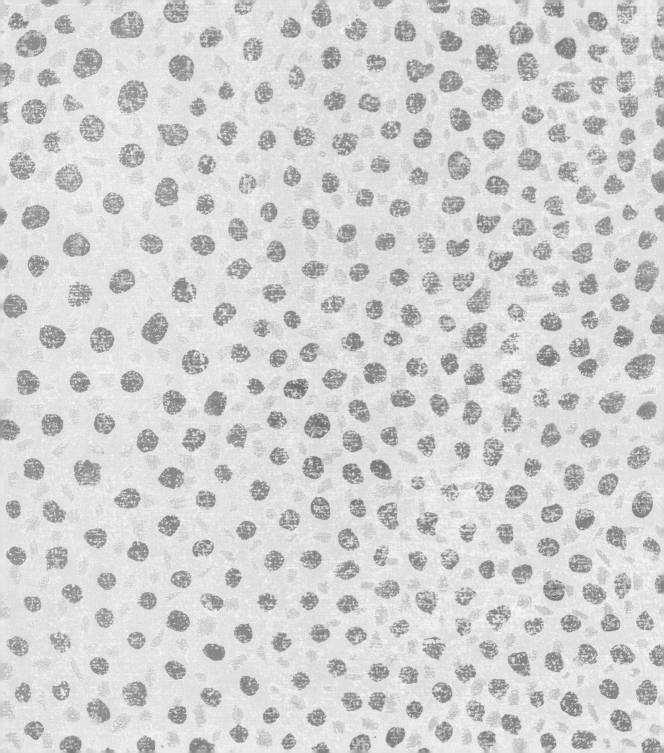